PICTURE PERFECT

SERENA PATEL

Illustrated by
Louise Forshaw

Barrington Stoke

First published in 2022 in Great Britain by
Barrington Stoke Ltd
18 Walker Street, Edinburgh, EH3 7LP

www.barringtonstoke.co.uk

Text © 2022 Serena Patel
Illustrations © 2022 Louise Forshaw

A CIP catalogue record for this book is available
from the British Library upon request

ISBN: 978-1-80090-090-5

Printed by Hussar Books, Poland

To Anu, Krupa and Varsha.

For all our perfectly imperfect family moments.

Chapter 1

It all started with the photo project Sonal had to do for school. They had to pick a theme for the project, and Sonal picked "Family". It felt like her family was always too busy these days. They never did anything together. Maybe, thought Sonal, if they all helped her with her project, they would get to spend some time together. It could even be fun.

And if her family had just been able to sit still and all look at the camera for five seconds, everything might have gone OK ...

The deadline for the project was next week, and Sonal wanted a group photo of her family to start the project off. But they were never in the same place at the same time – they were always too busy. And then, for once, this Friday night, everyone was in the living room together. It was the perfect moment for a lovely family picture.

But as Sonal tried to get everyone to sit in the right place and look at her camera, she could see this was not going to work. No one was paying any attention!

Mum and Dad were both on their phones as usual. They always had emails or messages coming in or else they were reading the news and looking at social media. Jay, Sonal's annoying little brother, wouldn't put down his console and kept shouting out "BOOM!" Reena, their elder sister, was typing away on her laptop and moaning at Sonal that there were more important things in the world than a photo.

"I have more important things to think about than your photo project, Sonal. What

about countries where there is war and no food? Do you think they do photo projects? What about climate change? Do you think we have time for this when the world is burning? You need to get real and get out more, Sonal!" Reena said as she jabbed Sonal's head with her finger. This kind of hurt, and it made Sonal's glasses fall lopsided on her face.

The family's new puppy, Jalebi, was yapping and jumping up into Sonal's lap as she tried to get her phone on the selfie stick and into the right place.

"Jalebi, not now!" Sonal shouted as Jalebi licked her face.

Nanna, Sonal's grandfather, sat down on the arm of the sofa with a groan. "Oh, my hip is playing up again. Right, where do you want me, Sonal? Here on the end?"

Sonal sighed. "Don't bother, Nanna. No one really wants to take a family photo. Why would they ever take an interest in something that's important to me?"

"Listen up, you lot!" Nanna said loudly. "Pay attention for just a moment, will you? This is important to our Sonal!"

Nanna never talked loudly. Everyone was surprised. They looked up and stopped what they were doing.

"At last!" Sonal said. "OK, ready? Everyone, say cheese!" Sonal held out the selfie stick and made sure everyone was in shot. But just as she got ready to press the button, Jalebi started whining.

"I think he needs a wee," Jay said.

"Just one more second and you can take him," Sonal muttered.

"Sis, he can't wait. He's a puppy!" Jay replied.

"Sit still, will you? I've almost got the shot!" Sonal said.

But it was too late. Jalebi stood up. There was a puddle of wee all over Sonal's lap.

"Eww!" Jay squealed, and jumped up.

"That is rank!" Reena snorted, and got up too.

"I'll get a towel, naughty pup!" Mum scolded, and went to the kitchen.

"Are you OK, love? Maybe best to do this later?" Dad said. He picked his phone back up and started to scroll down the screen again.

"Forget it," Sonal said as she grabbed some tissues to soak up the wee. "This project is doomed!"

Nanna put his arm round her. "Oh, diku," he said, which is what he always called her. It was Gujarati for "my child". Shall we leave it for now and get cleaned up? I'll make you a nice hot chocolate, and then you can tell me all about this project, huh?"

Sonal loved her nanna. He always knew how to make things better.

*

A little while later, Sonal and Nanna sat together in the kitchen in front of two mugs of hot chocolate and Nanna's special stash of biscuits.

"So, what is this project, Sonal?" Nanna asked kindly.

"Well, it's a photography project, and I chose family as the theme for mine. But I don't know why I bothered!" she sighed. "There's this girl at school, right? Her name is Dina Dawson, and she's chosen family for her theme too. She'll have the best project. It'll be all perfect family snaps, everyone smiling, all wonderful, and I can't even get my family to take one photo together!"

Dina was always showing off photos of her family trips – skiing, rock climbing, swimming in clear blue seas. Her pictures of life at home were great too – dog walks, baking amazing cakes and chilling out in cuddly matching jumpers. Sonal's life was never going to be like that.

"Oh, Sonal, never mind about this Dina girl. Don't compare yourself to others, diku. It's not a good path to go down," Nanna said, getting up from his seat. "Now, if the theme is family, how about we get out our old albums for some ideas?" He went over to one of the cupboards and pulled out a big box. "Here, look!"

"I haven't seen these for ages," Sonal said as she helped Nanna lift the heavy box onto the kitchen table.

Nanna smiled. "We don't get them out very often any more. Everyone in this family is too busy most of the time. But I like looking at them. They bring back lovely memories."

Sonal picked out a grey album with a silver leaf on the cover. It was heavy and looked full of photos. She turned the first page. "Is that ... Mum?" she asked as she pointed at a picture of a young girl smiling sweetly at the camera and holding hands with a little boy.

"Ah, yes! That's your mum and her brother, your uncle Ram."

"They must have been good friends. Jay would never hold hands with me like that!" Sonal said.

"Ha, don't believe everything you see in photos, diku. I remember taking this picture. Your grandmother had to promise them lollipops if they just stood still and smiled for two minutes. Right after I took the picture, your uncle pulled his hand away and kicked your mum, then she started crying!"

"Really? They look so happy in the picture. And look here at this one of you all sitting together smiling!" Sonal said. "I wish our family would sit like that for just one picture! It's so hard getting everyone together in one place."

"Things were different in the old days," Nanna said, and nodded. "Our lives weren't so busy all the time, and screens weren't so important. We only had one television in the house. No internet, no distractions. We ran around outside; we played board games. We even talked to each other – can you believe it?" he laughed.

"The old days sound kind of good, Nanna. No one in this family ever wants to play a board game, and even when we do, we have to let Jay win because he's the youngest! My project is just going to be pictures of you and me at this rate!"

"It can't be that bad. What photos do you have already? There's probably more good ones than you think," Nanna said.

Sonal pulled out her phone and scrolled through the pictures she'd already snapped. There was one of Dad, but he'd moved mid shot, so it was all blurry. Another of Jay and Reena, but they were facing opposite ways and both looking at their tablets. Here was one of Mum, but she was holding up one hand telling Sonal to wait as she was talking on her phone with the other. There were a few cute ones of Jalebi and a couple of nice selfies Sonal had taken of her and Nanna, but that was it. Not much of a family photo project.

"It's hopeless, I'm telling you, Nanna. I should just pick another theme. Maybe rocks? They don't look at screens, and they stay where you put them!"

Sonal picked up the photo album again. "Look at this picture – you look like you're all having fun here! And you're all looking in the same direction!" she said.

"Ah, that was taken on a camping trip. We only went camping once, but we had a very happy weekend. Your mum climbed a tree, if you can believe it!"

"Mum? My mum?" Sonal asked. "I *don't* believe it!"

Nanna laughed. "It happened and, you know what, she had the best time. Actually, that gives me an idea. This family could do with spending some time together doing something nice and remembering how much fun that can be. Plus, we might be able to get some really nice pictures for your project!"

Sonal half smiled. "So, what's the idea, Nanna?" she asked.

"Well, you said it yourself, we look so happy in this picture. How about we all go on a little camping trip this weekend?"

"Camping?" Sonal said. "I don't know if they'll agree to that."

"They're not going to have a choice!" Nanna said firmly. "Not only that but we're going to ban screens from the trip too."

"No screens all weekend? Really, Nanna? I'm not sure about that," Sonal said.

"We want everyone to enjoy the moment and have time together. I think no screens will help," Nanna said.

"I guess you're right. But they're really not going to like it!" Sonal giggled. "But wait a second – how will I take photos for the project if I don't have my phone?"

"I have a camera you can use," Nanna answered. "Now let's get the laptop and see about booking a campsite. We'll need some supplies too!"

"Are we really doing this?" Sonal asked.

"Yes, we are!" Nanna replied. "It's time the screens had a weekend off!"

Chapter 2

A little while later, Sonal and Nanna came out of the kitchen with Jalebi. All three looked very pleased with themselves.

Mum was in the front garden talking to her friend next door. Dad was on his phone speaking to someone about work. Reena was watching a YouTube video. Jay was pressing all the buttons on his console controller very quickly. He was playing that zombie game again that Mum hated because it gave him nightmares.

"Umm, I need everyone to listen to me for a moment," Sonal said.

Everyone carried on with what they were doing.

Sonal looked at Nanna, who sighed and shouted, "LISTEN UP! Sonal has something to say!"

That got them to pay attention. Even Mum came in from outside, asking, "What's all the shouting about?"

"Sonal has something important to say, and you're all going to listen, aren't you?" Nanna said.

"Do we have to?" Jay moaned.

"YES!" Nanna said sternly.

Everyone sat down and looked at Sonal. She felt sick. What if they laughed at the plan? But she knew she had to try. This was important.

Sonal stood at the front of the living room. "I want to show you something," she said. "As you know, I've been trying to take some family photos for my school project, and let's just say it hasn't been going so well."

"Really?" Dad asked. "Why?"

Sonal looked quickly over at Nanna. He nodded and smiled at her.

"Well, it's probably best you see for yourselves," Sonal said. "I've put some of the photos onto the tablet so you can see them a bit better."

She flicked through the pictures she'd transferred from her phone. The ones where Mum and Dad didn't look up from their phones; the ones that had turned out all blurry because no one would take the time to sit still; and the one where Jalebi had his accident. There was not one photo where everyone was looking at the camera.

Dad shifted in his seat. "OK, I mean, that last one would have been fine if not for Jalebi."

"And all the other photos would have been fine if you lot weren't always stuck to your screens," Sonal pointed out.

Nobody answered her.

"Well, anyway, here are some photos from when Mum was little. See if you can spot the difference," Sonal said, laying the album on the coffee table, open at the pictures of the camping trip.

Everyone looked.

"Wow, these pictures are old," Jay commented. "Mum, is that you?"

"Aw, I remember this trip!" Mum said, smiling at Nanna. "We had a fantastic time at that campsite."

"Yes, and when was the last time that we all spent some proper time together like that, Mum?" Sonal asked.

Reena yawned. "What's the big deal, Sonal? We see each other every day. We're always together!"

"You don't get it. Yeah – perhaps we see each other every day, but we don't do stuff together or even just sit and talk! That's the problem!" Sonal said.

"We're talking right now," Jay pointed out.

"You know what I mean, Jay. You're always playing on your console. Mum and Dad are always at work or on their phones. Reena's either not here or in our room on her laptop with the door shut. Nanna is the only person in this family I can talk to!"

Mum looked upset. "Sonal, you can talk to me and your father anytime."

"No, Mum, I can't! It's always: 'Just one second,' or 'Hang on a minute,' or 'Can we talk later?' Later never comes!"

"That's kind of true actually," Jay agreed, to Sonal's surprise.

"Now hang on, it's not true," Dad said, and then he looked at Mum. "Is it?"

"Well, I was talking about my rally the other day, and you weren't even listening," said Reena. "You think we don't notice when you just nod or agree, but we do know you haven't got a clue what we're talking about."

Sonal looked down at the floor. "I feel like everyone is so into their own stuff. We don't stop to listen to each other. I don't even feel like we're a family sometimes," she said.

Mum gasped. "Diku, of course we're a family. We're all just busy, I suppose."

"You're all so busy ALL the time!" Sonal pointed out. "So busy we can't even take one good photo together!"

"OK, what can we do to fix this?" Dad asked.

Nanna smiled. "Funny you should ask. We have a plan. We're all going camping!"

"A camping trip?" Mum said. "Oh, what a great idea! We can get something booked in for half-term."

"Ooh, half-term, I'm not sure I can get away then," Dad said.

"No, I've got a rally that week!" Reena protested.

"I don't think any of you understand," Sonal said. "The trip is an emergency family event, and it's happening this weekend."

Everyone burst out talking, and Sonal smiled to herself when she saw the panic on her parents' faces as they tried to think of a reason not to go camping.

"Umm, we don't have a tent!" Dad said.

"Ordered one just now. It'll be here tomorrow!" Nanna replied. "Next-day delivery!"

"Well, I've got that school meeting on Saturday morning!" Mum said.

"You can ring and say you can't go this time," Nanna answered.

"Yeah, but I've got that gaming tournament!" Jay piped up.

"There'll be other tournaments, and you could do with a break from that console thing anyway," Nanna said.

"You lot can go, but I'm going to that peaceful protest in the park, remember? I can't miss it," Reena said.

"Sometimes you have to tackle the things at home before you can go out and fight the world," Nanna said.

Reena went to open her mouth but couldn't think of anything to say, so she stayed quiet.

The whole family sat back and looked at Nanna and Sonal.

"I guess we're going camping!" Dad said. "Will that make you happy, Sonal?"

"Yes!" said Sonal.

Nanna smiled. "There's one more thing. I have a rule for our trip."

Everyone groaned.

"What rule? You're not going to make us do weird outdoor challenges, are you? I'm not eating fried slugs!" Jay said.

"Actually, entomophagy – eating insects – is very good for you and good for the environment!" Reena replied.

"And how many insects have you eaten, Reena?" Jay said, and stuck his tongue out at his sister.

Nanna cut in before they broke out into a real argument. "Listen, there's no bug eating, OK? It's just a small thing. For the trip to make a difference to our family, I want you all to leave all your screens and technology behind."

Sonal added, "At least then there's some hope of me getting some decent pictures for this photo project!"

There was a long silence and then, "The whole weekend? You have got to be kidding!" from Jay.

"You are having a laugh!" from Reena.

"But what about work? I might need to check my emails, diku!" from Dad.

"Well, I suppose a break might be nice. I could take some books to read!" from Mum.

"It's my rule and it's non-negotiable," Nanna said sternly. "It won't kill you all to have some screen-free time."

"It's just for two days," Sonal said. "If we can't switch off our phones, consoles and tablets for two days, then we've got a serious problem!"

The family thought for a moment.

"Aha! What about Jalebi?" Jay said. "We've only had him a few weeks. We can't take him camping, and he can't be left alone!"

Mum frowned. "Jay might have a point, sweetheart. Jalebi is still very little. I don't know what he'll be like out in the countryside and around other campers. Maybe we need to wait for a few more weeks before we all go camping?"

"No, Mum! I'll look after Jalebi, I promise! I'll make sure he's OK!" Sonal said.

Sonal looked so excited and hopeful that, after a few moments, Mum agreed. "OK, diku, we can go. All six of us and the dog – what can go wrong?" Mum laughed as she watched Jalebi pick up the TV remote in his mouth and try to eat it.

Chapter 3

The next morning the family woke up early to get ready for their camping trip. Nanna was right about next-day delivery. The tent came before ten o'clock, so there was no excuse not to go!

"This is going to be so great!" Sonal said to Reena as they packed their things. Sonal packed the camera Nanna had given her last night. It was heavy and black and called a Kodak PixPro.

Reena was packing books and baggy jumpers and grunted at Sonal. "I just want to get it over with and get back to my own

life. Do you realise you've spoiled my whole
weekend, and for what? So you can get a couple
of nice family snaps to show at school? It's all
fake, you know. When you see people's pictures
online or whatever, they're only showing you
what they want you to see. There's no such

thing as a perfect family." And with that, Reena stomped off downstairs with her bag.

Sonal sighed. She and Reena used to be good friends. A few years ago they would both have been excited about a trip away. But they'd drifted apart.

Reena was going to be sixteen soon, and she was always looking for something new to support or protest about. When Sonal tried to talk to her about normal stuff like TV programmes or school, Reena would just say that there were bigger things in the world to worry about, that Sonal's interests were silly. Sonal wished they could talk about the small stuff too. It felt like they had nothing in common any more.

Then Jay came in. He was cross with Sonal too.

"I hope you're happy. Making us go on this stupid trip. If I can't take my console, what am I supposed to do for fun? It's going to be so boring. We'll just be sitting around looking at sheep." And he stormed off.

Sonal remembered how they used to play together a lot when he was little. He always wanted her to draw stuff for him to colour in. But ever since he turned ten a few months ago, he'd become obsessed with gaming and just spent all his free time on his console.

"He's so dramatic!" Nanna laughed as he looked in at the girls' bedroom door. "Can I come in, diku?"

Sonal sighed. "Everyone hates me, Nanna. This is a great start to my project – not! All the photos will be of them giving me or each other angry looks!" she said.

"They'll cheer up, Sonal. Country air does something to the brain. Opens it up, brings calm and happiness! Your grandmother and I used to love hopping in the car and going for a trip out to the countryside."

"Really?" Sonal asked. "I wish she was here now. I miss her."

"Me too, diku, me too. But she wouldn't let anything stop her from getting the job done, and so we have to focus and not let a bunch of grumpy pantses get us down, OK?"

Sonal nodded. She was glad Nanna was on her side. He was right: she would bring the family together like she'd planned. This trip was going to be awesome, and then she'd have lots of great photos for her project!

*

The whole family piled into Mum's seven-seater people carrier, and two hours later, after much moaning, shoving, an accidental dog wee and lots of arguments, they arrived.

Tedsmore Lakes campsite was even prettier than it looked on the website. They were in a big field with trees all around them. Off to the right there was a lake, which glimmered in the sunlight. In front of them a few different-sized tents were already set up.

Sonal's family plot had a little sign on a piece of wood that said "GUPTA" on it.

"Is this it?" Jay asked. "There's nothing here!"

"Yeah, like what are we meant to do here?" Reena asked.

"Chill out, talk, play games, walk the dog, family time," Sonal replied, getting her camera out, ready to record every moment of their camping trip.

"Ugh, sounds BORING!" said Jay, flopping down onto the grass next to where Mum had parked their car.

"Well, we can start by putting up our tent, unless you want to sleep right there under the stars, son?" said Dad.

"Err, no thanks. I'd rather have some sort of roof over my head!" Jay said, jumping up. "But I need to go to the toilet first!"

"You always need the toilet when there's work to do!" Sonal pointed out.

"Come on," said Mum, "I need to go too, and we can check out the showers while we're there."

As Mum and Jay walked off towards the toilet block, Sonal noticed the most amazing tent across the way. It was huge, like a mini circus tent, and it had lights, bunting and an outdoor seating area.

Reena noticed it too and whistled. "Now that's a tent!"

"That's not camping!" Dad scoffed. "Real camping is hard on the back!"

"Err, why are we doing it then?" Reena asked.

"Can we just try to get our tent up, and then we'll admire that other one later?" Sonal said.

But at that very moment, a head poked out from the other tent. It was a girl about Sonal's age. No, it couldn't be ...

It was! The last person Sonal wanted to be camping right opposite. It was Dina Dawson!

"Hiiiiiii," Dina called out as she skipped over. She was wearing a shiny bomber jacket, T-shirt and shorts and what looked like expensive trainers. She looked annoyingly happy to see Sonal.

"Hi, Dina. How weird to see you here!" Sonal answered.

Dina grinned. "I know! Weird, right?"

Dina saw the rest of Sonal's family getting ready to put their tent up. She held out her hand to Sonal's dad.

"Hi, I'm Dina. I go to school with Sonal. I'm here with my family. Sonal, shall we hang out later? Oh, isn't your dog sweet? Are you on Instagram? My mum's an influencer. She gets to try out all the cool fashion and beauty brands. Look!"

Sonal didn't have a chance to answer any of Dina's questions as Dina had pushed her phone in front of Sonal's face and started to show her a screen full of happy family photos.

Every photo was perfectly posed and smiley. Ugh, everything Sonal's family photos weren't.

"Nice," was all Sonal could think of to say.

Dina asked Reena if they would like to come over for hot chocolate later, but Sonal jumped in, saying, "Umm, no thank you. We're going to get settled in today – maybe tomorrow?"

"That was nice of her to offer," Nanna commented as Dina skipped away.

"Yeah, I guess. I just want it to be us six for now," Sonal said.

Jalebi barked at her heels. "OK, OK, us seven." Sonal laughed.

Just then Mum and Jay came back from the toilet block. They were arguing.

"You can't not wash for the next two days!" Mum was saying.

"I am not showering in front of strangers!" Jay told her. "When you said showers, I didn't realise it would all be open like that!"

"It's probably just like at swimming and you can keep your shorts on, dummy!" Reena sighed.

"Er, let's speak nicely to each other, please," said Dad. "Now, how about helping me put this tent up? Then we can go for a walk and gather some firewood. That'll be fun!"

Jay made a face and Reena grunted, but they helped to get the tent out of the boot of the car.

The instructions said: "Easy to put up." Sadly, that was the easiest part to understand.

"So, this thing goes where?" Mum asked from under the tent cover, which she was trying to hold up in the air for the tent pole. "Not now, Jalebi!" she shouted as the puppy tried to get in under the tent too.

"Through this bit," Dad said. "Not here, there!"

"I can do it. Look!" Jay said as he poked the pole right through the tent material and made a great big rip in the roof.

"Oops!" Jay said as he hid his face behind the instruction sheet. Sonal thought it was funny, so she quickly took a picture before everyone moved.

After a lot of shouting and some bad words from the adults, the tent was up at last. Nanna said the hole in the roof made it special because now they had a window to the stars.

"As long as it doesn't rain," said Mum.

"It'll be fine," Nanna said. "Bit of rain never hurt anyone, did it? Let's go for that walk and get some wood for the fire."

"Do we have to?" Jay moaned.

"If you want something warm for dinner, then yes," Sonal warned.

With that, the family set off for a walk round the woods next to the campsite. At first everyone was complaining, especially when it seemed they had got themselves lost. Even Nanna said it might have been handy to have a phone to help them find their way!

But they soon got back on track, and it was actually quite fun seeing who could collect the biggest twigs. Until Jay conked himself in the head with a big stick while he was waving it around pretending it was a lightsaber.

There was another tricky moment when Sonal went under the fence to pick up a twig on the other side – and came face to face with a rather annoyed cow! They made a quick exit from that part of the field! And for the first time in ages they were all laughing and joking together. Sonal started to relax and enjoy herself.

But Reena still wasn't happy. "Do you see all this rubbish?" she shouted, pointing to drinks cans and bits of plastic that had been stuffed into a hedge rather than carried back to the bins. "People are so careless! Someone needs to do something!"

"Maybe you should!" Mum joked, but Reena grinned.

"Maybe I will!" Reena said.

Once they'd collected enough wood for the fire, the family went back to their tent, and Nanna got out the things he needed to cook for dinner.

It took a while to get the fire started with a flint and a bit of wood, but in the end Mum pulled out some fire-lighters and matches and started one that way.

"I would have got it if you'd just waited a bit longer," Dad moaned.

"We haven't got all night, Dad," Reena said.

"Right, who's helping me?" Nanna asked.

"I will!" Sonal said.

"OK, then the rest of you can make a nice eating area. There's some blankets in the car along with the plates and things," Nanna said.

Nanna chopped some onion and fried it in oil in a pan over the fire. He showed Sonal which spices to add – half a teaspoon of turmeric, a pinch of garam masala, two teaspoons of ground coriander and a sprinkling of salt. Then, when the onions were done, they added chopped potatoes and cauliflower and cooked them with the lid closed.

The smell of cauliflower and potato shaak wafted around them, and Sonal was starving by the time the food was ready. Nanna had brought a big batch of rotli with him too and a jar of his home-made pickle. Yum, yum!

Later, after they had all eaten and cleared away, the family sat just outside the tent looking up at the night sky.

"Does anyone know what we're looking at?" Mum asked.

"That's Orion's belt, I think!" Dad said.

"No, it's Ursa Major," Jay said in a very matter-of-fact way. "If I had my phone, I could prove it to you with my star-finding app!" He looked pointedly at Nanna.

Mum said, "I'm sure you're both right."

"How can they both be right?" Sonal asked.

Dad coughed loudly. "Well, anyway," he said. "Isn't it lovely just to be here and have this view?"

"Exactly!" Nanna agreed. "You know, when I was a boy back in India, the roof of our house was flat. You could sleep up there. We used to drag our mattresses out and sleep under the stars! We didn't need any apps to identify the stars either. My nanna gave me a top tip for how to find Orion's belt, you know. You have to look for the hourglass shape of Orion and then the three stars in a row that create the narrow part of the hourglass. Those are the ones that form Orion's Belt."

"That's amazing," Sonal said as she tried to imagine Nanna as a boy.

"It was amazing until the mosquitoes got us. We had to put up nets to stop them drinking all our blood!" Nanna said.

Jay thought for a moment. "Are there mosquitoes here?" he asked.

Reena snorted, "Yeah, monster-sized ones!"

"Reena!" Dad scolded.

Sonal smiled to herself. She couldn't remember the last time they'd sat around like this just chatting and laughing together. It was nice. Quietly she pulled out the camera and took a picture of her family as they sat looking up at the twinkling night sky.

A little while later they were all tired and decided to turn in for the night. But this turned out to be a BIG problem. Although Nanna had ordered a family tent, it was only big enough for a family of four rather than six plus a dog.

It was a tight squeeze when they all tried
to lie down. Reena got a foot in the face, and
no one was sure whose foot it was because they
were all so squished.

After a lot of banging of elbows and knees, groans and ouches, Mum and Dad decided to take their sleeping bags to the people carrier and sleep in there.

Nanna tucked all the children in even though they were way too old for all that now. But no one complained, Sonal noticed. Even Jalebi snuggled down next to Sonal and fell asleep right away, which he never did at home. The country air had worn him out. She'd just let him sleep here next to her rather than in his crate, she thought.

As her eyes started to close, Sonal thought back over the day. There had been ups and downs, but maybe, just maybe, this trip would work out OK after all.

Chapter 4

The next morning Sonal was woken by a loud shout. "What the ...?!"

She grabbed her glasses and shoved them on, rolled out of her sleeping bag and poked her head out of the tent, almost headbutting Dad's leg.

"Dad, what are you doing?" she asked.

"That puppy!" Dad yelled. "Sonal, did you take him for a walk last night?"

"Oops, I forgot with all the fuss of putting up the tent," Sonal said. "And then he fell asleep so quickly!"

"Well, I think Jalebi took himself for a walk this morning, but he didn't go far because I've just stepped in his doggy do-do!" Dad growled. "You said you would look after him, Sonal. I'm not seeing that right now! He should have been put in his crate last night!"

Sonal made a face as she saw that the bottom of Dad's sandal was now covered in smelly squelchy brown stuff. Oh, Jalebi!

Nanna, Reena and Jay popped their heads out of the opening in the tent above Sonal. "What's going on?" Jay asked. "Oh, Dad, that stinks!" he said, pinching his nose.

"Great start to my day this is!" Dad muttered as he shook off his sandal and hopped to the shower block.

It had rained in the night, so the tent and everything in it was a bit soggy. Grumpily, they all got dressed and went to the shower block to brush their teeth. As the children were walking back together to the tent, they saw Dina running towards them.

"Hiiiiii," she squealed. "Did you sleep well? Our tent was so comfortable! Do you want to come over and watch a movie later? Dad's got this projector, and we're going to watch a scary movie tonight! You can meet my two brothers."

"Cool!" Jay said.

Sonal nudged him. "Err, no, we've promised to spend time together as a family," she said. "We've made a no-screen pact for this weekend, and that includes movies."

"Oh, wow! No screens at all?" Dina exclaimed. "I don't know what I would do without my phone! OK, well, if you change your mind, we're only over there!" She smiled and ran back to her tent.

"She was just trying to be nice, Sonal. You were pretty rude," Reena said, walking off ahead.

"You're sucking the small amount of fun there is out of this trip, Sonal," Jay moaned, and then he ran after Reena.

Sonal's eyes stung. She'd show them! This trip could be fun, and they didn't need Dina and her posh projector. She'd start by making everyone a tasty breakfast.

So while the others took Jalebi for a quick morning walk round the campsite, Nanna and Sonal got the sausages and bread out and started a fire to cook them on.

"You're not saying much," Nanna commented as he turned the sausages. "Everything OK?"

"Yeah, I guess," Sonal answered. "I just wish being part of a family was easier."

Nanna chuckled. "Easy? No, diku, families are not easy. But families are the friends you don't get to choose."

"Well, I'm sure Reena and Jay don't think I'm their friend. They think I'm sucking all the fun out of their lives," Sonal said with a shrug.

"Don't listen to them, diku," Nanna told her. "They are off having a walk, aren't they? And I bet they're enjoying it even if they won't admit it. Didn't they have fun last night? There was laughter," he pointed out.

Sonal was about to agree when she spotted something over Nanna's shoulder. It was Jalebi! He'd obviously slipped off his lead and was bounding over to Dina and her family, who were also making breakfast. It looked like Dina's mum was trying to take the perfect photo of the scene, getting Dina to pose with the frying pan in one hand and a chef's hat on her head. Her two brothers were pulling faces at her from behind their mum.

"Jalebi, come here!" Sonal called out.

Nanna turned to look. "He's heading for their breakfast!" he exclaimed. "I'll get him."

Sonal jumped up too, and they ran across the field.

They were too late. Jalebi got there first and was yapping at Dina and her family. As Sonal approached, she could see he had a piece of bacon hanging from his mouth. "Jalebi, no!" she shouted.

Jalebi ignored her and ran back towards Nanna, but the puppy had somehow caught his leg in the end of the other family's bunting. As he ran, he pulled the bunting with him and it broke away from where it had been tied. Jalebi

kept running, dragging the bunting behind him across the field.

"That photo was going to be perfect, and now look, it's all ruined!" Dina's mum cried, pointing to the eggs and what was left of the bacon lying on the ground. Dina was looking upset, and her two brothers rolled about laughing.

"I'm so sorry!" Sonal said. "We'll ... umm ... return your bunting. Sorry again!" And she ran after Jalebi before they could say anything else.

Nanna had picked up Jalebi and was undoing the bunting string, which was all tied around him. Jalebi was trying to eat his stolen piece of bacon and wriggling, so it looked really funny.

Sonal didn't know why, but she grabbed her camera and took a picture.

"Let's get this fella into his crate and make sure we shut the door properly. He seems to be a little escape artist!" Nanna said as they walked back to their own tent.

Sonal was doing just that when she heard the rest of the family returning and Nanna telling them that they'd caught the puppy.

"What's that smell?" Jay complained.

Sonal sniffed. "Oh no, the sausages!" She left Jalebi in his crate and ran over to the little outdoor grill they had been cooking on, but it was too late. The sausages were burnt black.

"Oh man, I was looking forward to those!" Jay complained. "Trust Sonal to burn the breakfast."

"It wasn't my fault," Sonal huffed.

"You were the one who wanted to make breakfast," Reena said.

"Calm down, everyone!" said Nanna. "I can easily whip up one of my special omelettes. It won't take long. Why don't you all play a game of rounders while I cook? Go on, the exercise will work up your appetite."

"I've already been for a walk!" Jay grumbled.

"Can't we play a board game instead?" Mum asked.

"Monopoly?" Dad suggested.

"NO! You know what happens every time we play that – it always ends in tears," Sonal said.

"It's a game based on money and power; I'm not playing that," Reena said firmly, crossing her arms.

"You used to like it when you were younger," Nanna said, and shrugged.

"You know what, let's just try rounders. It'll be fun, and I can take a couple of nice photos for my project!" Sonal said.

In the end, Jay and Reena agreed, so while Nanna started mixing eggs for the omelette, Mum and Dad set out jackets for the bases and found the rounders bat and ball from the car. Luckily the ground had dried out a bit, so it wasn't too muddy now.

Sonal was up first to bat, and Jay was bowling. But he threw the ball too high, and Sonal couldn't see it because the sun was in her eyes.

"Jay! Throw it properly!" Sonal yelled.

"That *was* properly!"

"It wasn't, and now look, the ball is all the way over there. You'll have to get it."

"You get it!"

"Someone fetch it!" Dad shouted.

As if on cue, Jalebi came darting out of the tent at that exact moment!

"How did he get out?" Dad yelled. "SONAL?"

Sonal gulped. She hadn't closed the crate properly because she had smelled the sausages burning. And now Jalebi had the ball and was running, fast, away from their tent and out into the campsite.

"Quick, we need to catch him!" Mum said.

"This is all down to you, Sonal," Jay yelled. "If anything happens to him, it'll be your fault! This whole trip has been horrible," he said, staring right at Sonal.

"I don't exactly want to be here either," Reena said.

Sonal's cheeks felt hot. She was getting so sick of everyone complaining. Suddenly she was shouting, "Do you know what? It would have been better if we'd never come on this trip. No one wants to be here, and I've got rubbish photos so far anyway. I'll get Jalebi. It's my fault that he's escaped. Don't bother following me."

Sonal dropped the bat and stomped away to find Jalebi.

Stupid holiday, stupid family, stupid photo project, stupid her for thinking it could ever be different.

Chapter 5

After a short distance, Sonal slowed down and took a deep breath. Maybe they should just give up and go home. The trip had been a bad idea. Who was she kidding anyway? She should have realised her family was never going to be picture perfect. And now Jalebi had run off, making it a proper disaster. She was pretty sure something like this could never happen to Dina Dawson.

Sonal felt fed up. She looked around for Jalebi, but she couldn't see him anywhere. Then she spotted Dina and her family on the lake in a little boat.

Dina's mum was standing up, trying to take a selfie, a perfect Insta picture. But Dina and her dad weren't looking, and her two brothers seemed to be arguing about something.

One brother was waving his oar around, and the mum started wobbling about. Suddenly the boat tilted up, and before anyone could stop it, they were all in the water!

Sonal ran to the edge of the lake to help the family out as they waded back to shore. They were completely soaked and not very happy at all.

"Are you OK?" she asked. "We have extra towels to dry off with if you need them?"

"No, we'll be OK," said Dina, sounding embarrassed. "We just need to get back to the tent, but thanks anyway."

Sonal watched the five of them walk away. One of the brothers was grumbling loudly. "I was trying to say we needed to go towards the trees!"

"You boys are a nightmare! I was trying to take a nice selfie for my social media!" Dina's mum said.

"Not every moment has to be on Instagram, dear," said Dina's dad.

"It would be nice just to enjoy being here," Dina added. "You know, without having to pose all the time?"

Sonal couldn't help but smile. Maybe they weren't such a perfect family after all.

She sat back down on the bench, thinking about her own family and everything that had happened. She felt bad for shouting at them. Maybe she should go back and apologise.

She watched as other families walked past. Two dads with their son carrying fishing rods and bait buckets. A girl and an older woman wearing matching Granny and Granddaughter jumpers. All kinds of different families living different lives. Were any of them perfect?

Just then Dad came along.

"I'm so sorry," said Sonal. "I didn't close the crate properly, and now I can't find him anywhere. Dad, Jalebi will be OK, won't he?" she cried.

Dad wrapped her in a big bear hug. "Don't worry. He's probably digging a hole to put that ball in somewhere nearby. The others are looking too. Between us we'll find him."

Chapter 6

Sonal and Dad went back and looked all around the tent and the car to see if Jalebi had come back. Nanna and Jay had gone to the edge of the field to make sure he hadn't run towards the road. Mum and Reena walked round the lake to see if he was having a paddle there.

Sonal felt awful. "I really am sorry, Dad. I didn't mean for this weekend to be so horrible," she said as they looked in the tall grass and behind trees.

"Sweetheart, it was a good idea. Perhaps we all haven't been as keen as we could have been.

We don't want you to feel we aren't a family. It upset us to hear that," Dad admitted.

"I didn't mean to upset you or Mum. I just feel like everyone has so much going on in their lives that we never do anything together. I just

thought if we spent some time together, we'd get on better, feel closer."

Dad laughed.

"It's not funny!" Sonal said, annoyed.

"It sort of is funny, diku," Dad said. "You see, I have four brothers, and I also felt like we drifted apart as we all got older."

"But you all have a great time together when we have family parties," Sonal said, thinking of the last family party when her uncles and dad had danced around in a circle to bhangra music.

"Ah yes, but when we were boys, my brothers were all into sports – cricket, football, rugby – which I hated. So I was always by myself in my room listening to music. That was what I loved. They all thought I was odd. But I didn't care. Well, maybe I cared a little bit. I wished they liked music too, but they didn't care about all that. Anyway, in the end,

I worked out we were a normal family, diku. All busy doing our own thing, with our different interests, sometimes falling out, but you know what? When I need a hand with something, or when my parents died, we worked together and helped each other."

Sonal nodded. Maybe her family wasn't such a disaster after all.

Suddenly she spotted a paw print in the mud. "Dad, look!" she shouted. "And here – another one!"

They followed the paw prints round the corner, and behind a tree there was a very muddy, very yappy Jalebi.

"What a mucky pup you are!" laughed Dad. "This is family life, Sonal – messy and full of surprises, mostly not picture perfect!" Dad picked up Jalebi and right away he had mud all over him.

A bit later, the family were all together by the edge of the lake with their crusty muddy pup, lots of towels, a bucket and a sponge.

"Right, how do we do this?" Dad asked.

"Just carry him in?" Mum suggested.

"Then I'll be all wet too!" Dad complained.

"Ha, well, you could kind of use a wash too, Dad. You smell of muddy dog," Jay said, giggling and holding his nose.

"Oh, I do, do I? How about you?" Dad grinned.

"Um, no, I smell fine," Jay said.

"I don't think you do. I think you need a wash too!" Dad yelled, chasing after Jay, then picking him up and walking to the water like he was going to dunk him.

"Nooooooooo!" Jay squealed.

Reena was laughing her head off. Mum grinned and flicked some water at her.

"MUUUUM!" Reena cried. "Not fair!"

Sonal snorted and then stopped when Reena turned to look at her. "So you think it's funny, do you? Come here and laugh!" Reena said with a big smile on her face, kicking water at Sonal.

Soon everyone was splashing water at each other and very out of breath. Jalebi, however, was still very muddy.

"Right, well, we're all wet, so we might as well get in and wash him properly," Nanna said.

The family splashed deeper into the water, and Jay held Jalebi while the others helped wash

him. Jalebi kept wriggling free and running out of the water back onto the muddy bank, so they had to chase him, bring him back and start again. It was hard work!

Sonal grabbed her camera and took lots of pictures of the family. Everyone was messy and soggy and no one stopped to pose, but Sonal had a feeling the photos would turn out to be her best work yet.

Chapter 7

Once Jalebi was finally clean and dry, the family made a plan to make the most of the rest of their trip.

"Are you sure you don't want to just go home? I know this weekend hasn't been great so far," Sonal said softly.

"Sis, it's cool. I don't mind staying." Jay smiled. "When we were looking for Jalebi, I met the brother of that girl, Dina, and he invited me to have a kickabout. I mean, we could all go if you like? You're good with the ball!"

Sonal smiled. "That could be fun," she said. "Oh but, Reena, you don't like football. We don't have to ..."

Reena grinned. "It's OK. I'll come. It might be a laugh, and then later we're all going to take part in a big litter pick of the fields. We saw all the rubbish around the campsite, and when we were looking for Jalebi, I spoke to the owner. She said it was a great idea. All the families are taking part."

Sonal looked her brother and sister up and down slowly. "Umm, what's going on? Why are you both being so nice?"

Reena shrugged. "Well, Dad had a word with us just now. We didn't know how bad you were feeling, and maybe you're right about us not spending much time together. I guess none of us noticed because we're all so busy with our own stuff all the time. I'm not saying this has been the best weekend ever, but it hasn't ALL been terrible."

Nanna put his arm around Sonal. "Looks like you got the family together after all!"

So once they had all eaten their breakfast omelette, they decided to go over to Dina's family's tent and play football with her brother.

It turned out that spending time with another family was fun, and Sonal enjoyed chatting with Dina, who was a middle sister too and got just as annoyed with her family. Somehow talking about it made the problems that seemed so big at home feel much smaller.

"I told my mum I don't like having to do the Instagram stuff all the time," Dina said.

"I thought you loved it?" Sonal replied.

"It's fun when she gets free stuff, but posing for photos and having to look great for every shot is rubbish! I feel like we don't get to just have normal family time," Dina sighed. "Not like your family. You're so lucky you just get to be you."

"I guess I never thought of it like that," Sonal admitted.

*

Later, Sonal sat with her camera and flicked through the pictures she'd taken. They were messy and sometimes out of focus, action packed and full of the crazy moments they'd shared so far. They could only belong to her family, and they were actually pretty perfect.

Just then, Jay came over. "We're gonna play a game before we go on Reena's clean-up walk. Wanna join in?"

"Sure, what are we playing?" Sonal asked.

"Monopoly! Even Reena said she'll play!" Jay grinned.

Sonal laughed. "Yeah, why not, what could possibly—" But before she could finish, Jalebi dashed past with lots of Monopoly money sticking out of his mouth ...

Our books are tested
for children and young people by
children and young people.

Thanks to everyone who consulted on
a manuscript for their time and effort in
helping us to make our books better
for our readers.